At the Park

Written by Annemarie Young
Illustrated by Louise Redshaw

WAYLAND

We saw a brown duck
at the park.

Park

We saw a white dog
at the park.

We saw a black bird
at the park.

9

We saw a red kite
at the park.

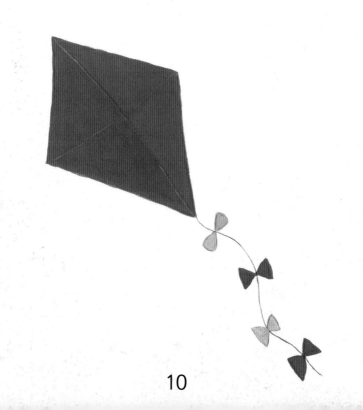

11

We saw a yellow hat
at the park.

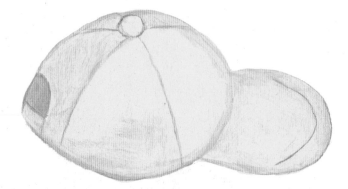

We saw a blue butterfly
at the park.

We saw a pink flower at the park.

We saw a green leaf at the park.

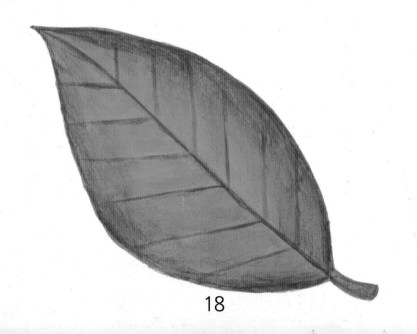

We saw a green
caterpillar on the leaf!

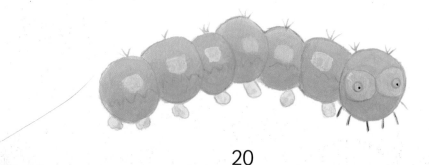

21

Guiding a First Read of
At the Park

It is important to talk through the book with the child before they read it alone. This prepares them for the way the story unfolds, and allows them to enjoy the pictures as you both talk naturally, using the language they will later encounter when reading. Read the brief overview below, and then follow the suggestions:

1. Talking through the book
The family went for a walk and they saw lots of different coloured things at the park.

Let's read the title: **At the Park**
Now turn to page 4. Here is the family.
What could they see on the water?
The family said, "We saw a brown
duck at the park."
Let's look at the next page.
What did the family see here?
Yes, it's a white dog. What do you think they said? Yes, "We saw a white dog at the park."

Continue through the book, guiding the discussion to fit the text as the child looks at the illustrations.

On page 18, the family said, "We saw a green leaf at the park." And on the last page, what was on the leaf? Yes, a green caterpillar!